CLEOPATRA'S CARPET

by KAREN WALLACE
illustrated by Alan Wade

Collins

An imprint of HarperCollinsPublishers

First published in Great Britain by Collins 2000
Collins is an imprint of HarperCollins*Publishers* Ltd,
77-85 Fulham Palace Road,
Hammersmith, London W6 8JB

The HarperCollins web site address is
www.**fire**and**water**.com

1 3 5 7 9 8 6 4 2

ISBN 0 00 675508 9

Printed and bound in Great Britain by
Omnia Books Limited, Glasgow

For Annie Nethercott

Chapter One

"Have you heard the news?" said Sophie Powers to her best friend Helen Murray, as the two girls walked down to the bus stop on their way to school.

"About Rhona McVeigh's Fancy Dress Disco?" said Helen, glumly.

Sophie shook her head. "About Mrs Trollope."

Mrs Trollope was their history teacher. She was very old-fashioned and had an amazing knack of making whatever she taught so boring, it was almost impossible not to fall asleep. This term they were doing a project on Cleopatra and as far as Helen was concerned, the whole thing was as dry as an Egyptian desert.

"What about her?"

"She fell off a ladder and broke both her legs," said Sophie in a rush. "So there's a new teacher starting this morning. Aunt Mary told me."

Sophie's Aunt Mary worked in the school office. She was better than a listening device any day.

"So who's the new teacher?" asked Helen.

Sophie shrugged. "I don't know. I just hope they don't get Mr Leadbetter out of retirement." She giggled. "He must be almost as old as Cleopatra."

Helen laughed. "Older."

At that moment the bus arrived and

they climbed on. Nigel Thimbleby was
sitting on the back seat. Helen stared at
Nigel's curly red hair and heavy black
glasses. For some reason he made Helen
feel more nervous than anyone else in the
class.

This was strange because he never said
anything and spent most of his time with
his nose buried in a book.

Maybe Nigel made her nervous because,
like her, he had red hair. And no matter
what anyone said, things were different if
you were a redhead.

As Helen headed down the bus, Nigel
looked up, blushed and
looked down again.

Sophie swung into a
pair of empty seats and
Helen followed with her
eyes firmly on her feet.

"Let's have a bet," said Sophie.

"What on?" replied Helen, who was delighted to have something else to think about.

"What the new teacher's like."

"What's the bet?" asked Helen.

Sophie looked around. The bus was just passing their favourite ice-cream bar. "How about a Big Fudge ice cream at Toni's?"

"OK." Helen pressed her lips together. "I bet the new teacher will be a man. He'll wear corduroy trousers, have a bald head and say, 'Now where was I?' a lot."

Sophie crossed her arms. "I bet it's a woman. She'll have straight hair, a face like an axe—" Sophie burst out laughing. "And hairy legs."

The bus stopped outside the school and they all got off. Five minutes later, Sophie and Helen and the rest of the class were sitting behind their desks waiting for the new history teacher to come in.

"Yum, yum," whispered Sophie. "I can just taste that Big Fudge ice cream."

Helen grinned shook her head. "No, you can't. *I* can."

At that moment the door opened and a woman walked into the room. She had a round rosy face and long hair loosely piled on her head. Silver hoops hung from her ears and half a dozen strings of beads glittered around her neck.

She wore a full flowery calf-length skirt and a soft blue shawl that was pinned at the front with a brooch in the shape of a crescent moon.

She perched on the side of the desk. "Hello, everyone," she said. "My name's Clarity Weaver. I'm your new history teacher and I want us all to be friends."

There was silence in the room. Some people stared at their desks. Others stared out the window. Some smirked behind their hands. Others, including Helen Murray and Nigel Thimbleby, went bright red.

There was only one thing worse than a history teacher and that was a history teacher who wanted to be friends.

Sophie rolled her eyes. "Come back, Mrs Trollope," she whispered. "All is forgiven."

"This is awful," muttered Helen to Sophie during lunch break. She took a bite of a chocolate bar. Even though it was her favourite kind she could hardly swallow it. "What am I going to do?"

As far as Helen was concerned, things couldn't have been worse. For most of the lesson Mrs Weaver waffled on about how history was about people and history projects were about teamwork. Then five minutes before the end, she dropped her bombshell. She had an exciting new idea. Wouldn't it be fun to do a history project in a different way? Of course it would!

Mrs Weaver put two boxes on the desk. Inside one were all the boys' names written on slips of paper. Inside the other were all the girls' names. Mrs Weaver would pick out one name from each box and split the class into teams of two. Then

each team would work on their history project together.

Mrs Weaver beamed. That way different people would each get to know each other and find out about Cleopatra at the same time!

All of the class felt as one. They didn't like the idea. They had already decided who was working with who. Why couldn't Mrs Weaver leave things alone?

But Mrs Weaver had a will of iron. She laughed in a silvery-bell voice and began to draw names from the boxes. Five minutes later, Helen was teamed up with Nigel Thimbleby.

Ten minutes earlier she had been planning a visit to London with Sophie. Apart from the Egyptian Rooms at the British Museum, there were a lot of rather good clothes shops they wanted to see.

Sophie patted her friend's arm. "It won't be as bad as you think," she said. "Nigel's all right really."

Helen sighed. "I know he's all right. It's just…" she shrugged. "How can I work with someone I can't talk to? All we do is blush at each other."

"How about hand signals?" Sophie pulled a face. "Anyway, you should count yourself lucky. There are more girls than boys so I've got Rhona McVeigh, Miss Moviestar 2010."

At that moment, Rhona McVeigh wandered over. Her glossy brown hair was pinned up with lots and lots of coloured clips and somehow her uniform looked like high fashion.

"Hi, Rhona," said Sophie. "Thanks for the invitation to your fancy-dress disco."

"Yeah, thanks," echoed Helen.

Rhona twirled her hair. "Oh, that's OK. Everybody's coming."

Rhona smiled at Sophie. "I'm really excited about the history project." She paused. "What do you think about doing a play?"

"What kind of play?" asked Sophie.

Rhona shrugged. "I dunno but I'll be Cleopatra and you can be that Roman general, whatshisname."

Helen hid a smile. Maybe Sophie was right.

Maybe she was better off with Nigel Thimbleby. At least he didn't think he was a mega star.

"You mean Mark Anthony," said Sophie. "The one with the muscly arms and the black curly hair."

"Yeah, him," said Rhona.

Sophie looked down at her hands and seemed to be thinking. "I could always wear arm bands and a wig," she said with a straight face.

Rhona's big brown eyes opened wide. "Wow! Could you really?"

Helen turned round so Rhona couldn't see her smiling.

And came face to face with Nigel Thimbleby.

They both went red.

"Let's buy a coke and discuss your costume," said Sophie to Rhona quickly.

"Helen and Nigel have things to talk about."

Rhona's face lit up like a candle. "Brilliant," she gushed. "I know exactly what I'm going to wear."

Sophie grinned and took her by the arm. "I thought you might."

Nigel and Helen stood staring at their feet.

Then Nigel twitched and looked up. "I was wondering if you could come to my house after school," he mumbled in a rush. "You see, my great-great-grandfather was an archaeologist in Egypt and, well, there's all this stuff in the attic."

Helen stared at him. "You mean stuff from Egypt?"

"I don't know." Nigel shrugged. "I was going to look through it on my own. But that was before Mrs Weaver..."

He stopped and stared at his feet again.

"Yeah," said Helen, knowing exactly what he meant. "Pity Mrs Trollope had to climb that ladder."

Something like a smile appeared on Nigel's face. It was as though they shared a secret. Neither of them liked the teamwork idea but they knew they had to get on with it.

"So can you come today?" asked Nigel. "My mum's away but Dad's around. He works in a shed in the garden."

"I'm sure I can," said Helen quickly. "I'll have to phone home but…" She smiled back. "There won't be a problem."

It was absolutely fine. Mrs Murray was delighted to hear about the team project. What a good idea! Helen needed to meet new people. Nigel Thimbleby was such a nice boy. Wasn't his father a writer? Anyway, they only lived in the next street so Helen could come home when she wanted.

And that was how Helen found herself knocking on Nigel Thimbleby's front door that afternoon after school.

Chapter 2

From the moment Nigel opened the door, Helen could feel that everything about his house was different from hers. There was old-fashioned wallpaper, and no carpet on the floor. Books were piled everywhere.

In Helen's house, everything was tidy. Everything matched and all the floors had wall-to-wall carpet.

"The attic's this way," said Nigel, trying furiously not to blush. They passed a grandfather clock with its hands on midnight. On either side two modern paintings hung crookedly on the wall.

Helen followed Nigel up two flights of bare wooden stairs with curly painted banisters. The stair rail was smooth from

years
and years of
hands rubbing up
and down it.

As she climbed the ladder
up to the attic, a fizzy excited
feeling flickered across her stomach.
She felt silly but the truth was Helen had
never been in a proper attic before. All the
attics she knew had been turned into extra
bedrooms or bathrooms.

Helen poked her head through the
opening and her heart leapt. Everything
looked exactly as she had hoped. The room
was long and followed the shape of the

pitched roof. A old wind-up gramophone stood balanced on top of a crooked stack of boxes. Rolled up carpets were piled in one corner beside a wooden rocking horse and a dolls' house with a tiny rooster weathervane. In the middle where the attic was highest was a huge wooden wardrobe. Glittery dresses and old-fashioned suits hung over its open double doors. Around the walls there were broken carriage lamps, loops of rope and dusty velvet curtains. There was even an enormous stuffed fish in a glass box.

The more Helen stared, the harder her heart thumped in her chest. "It's brilliant," she cried. "Absolutely brilliant."

Nigel smiled shyly. "It's my favourite place."

"If I had a place like this, I'd spend all my spare time in it," cried Helen.

Nigel looked up and grinned.

"I do."

To her amazement, Helen grinned back.
Then her eyes caught the glittery dresses
hanging over the wardrobe door.

Suddenly she blurted out something that
had been nagging at her all day. "I hate
going to fancy-dress discos," she said. "I
hate meeting new people, it's bad
enough at my sailing club."

Nigel's face lit up. "So
do I," he said. "I feel
really stupid."

As if he didn't want to lose the unexpected friendship, Nigel quickly pulled out an old carpet for them to sit on. "Dad says this is a Turkish carpet," he said, as he dragged it on to the floor. "They had ones like it in Cleopatra's time."

Helen took a corner and helped him spread the carpet out. A sweet smoky smell of sandalwood filled the room. The carpet had a strange design. Helen had never seen anything like it. First it looked as if it was covered in rose petals.

Then you could see ribbons of fruit and vegetables curling over and under swan-necked Roman fighting boats. Around the sides there were pictures of wild boar roasting over fires. And in the middle a Queen sat sideways on her throne.

Helen knelt down and looked more closely. A golden disc was in the Queen's hands.

"That's supposed to be something to do with Isis," said Nigel, pointing to the disc.

"Who's Isis?"

"She's an Egyptian goddess," explained Nigel.

Helen turned and saw something that was round and metal propped up in a corner.

"Hey! Look at that!" She picked it up and carried it back to the carpet. "It looks just like the one that Queen is holding."

"Except it's not golden," said Nigel.

"Maybe it's just dusty," replied Helen in a pretend mysterious voice. She sat down and rubbed it with her sleeve.

And that's when the strangest thing began to happen.

Afterwards neither Nigel nor Helen could remember which had started to spin first. The room or the carpet.

"I don't believe this," muttered Helen. Around them the attic was a blur of different colours.

As she said it, she was surprised that she wasn't a bit frightened.

"It *is* rather extraordinary," agreed Nigel as if he was looking at some kind of peculiar beetle.

Everything went faster and faster and
faster.

Helen remembered zipping the metal
disc into the front pocket of her hooded
top. It seemed like a good idea at the
time.

Then everything went black and silver. It
felt as if they were falling in a deep dark
sky through a shower of shooting stars.

It was hot and pitch black. Helen thought
later it was like being inside some kind of
loose woolly cocoon. They were lying, one
at either end, with their feet touching. And

they were moving up and down, up and down.

All around was the sound of creaking wood. The smell of sandalwood was so strong, it made you want to sneeze.

"I think we're inside that carpet," whispered Helen.

"So do I," whispered Nigel. "And I think we're on a boat."

As he spoke, his mind was racing. What boat? Where? When?

"Are you all right?" he whispered to Helen. "I mean you're not frightened or anything?"

"Nope," replied Helen matter of factly. "Just a bit hot."

"Me too." As he spoke, Nigel began to wriggle towards the end of the rolled up carpet. "I'm getting out of here."

"I'm coming, too."

Chapter 3

Nigel blinked and stared around him. It was definitely a boat.

He could see the wooden ribs under his feet. Now that he wasn't wrapped up in the carpet, the noise of the water rushing underneath the hull sounded eerily loud.

The only light came from tiny slits in the side of the boat. They were too narrow for Nigel to see anything outside, but there was enough light to show him stacks and stacks of tall pottery jars jammed between woven baskets.

He was standing in some kind of storage locker.

At that moment Helen appeared like a caterpillar out of her end of the carpet. "I can smell apricots," she whispered. She felt her way to the nearest jar and sniffed. It was stuffed with apricots. "Fancy one?"

Nigel grinned despite himself. Helen was incredibly brave. "Yes please."

Helen handed him an apricot and bit into one herself. It tasted quite unlike any apricot she had eaten before. It was as sweet and fragrant as wild-flower honey. She ate another one.

For a moment the two of them munched in silence. Everything was so extraordinary and unreal, neither of them knew what to say.

"It was something to do with that carpet," said Nigel at last.

"And the disc," said Helen. She patted the pocket of her top. "I thought we might need it again."

Nigel laughed edgily. "We're going to need something, that's for sure."

Helen looked all around. "We've got to get out of here."

"I know."

There was a trap door above them. Helen stood up and pushed it.

"Locked," she muttered.

At that moment, heavy footsteps clumped overhead. A deep voice shouted an order. "Bring the carpet immediately. Queen Cleopatra's orders."

Helen and Nigel stared at each other

with eyes as wide as saucers. But before either could speak, a bolt shot back. Then another.

"Hurry," croaked Helen. "This is our chance."

Nigel nodded. Then the two of them wriggled back into the rolled up carpet as fast as they could.

It was an uncomfortable ride. To stop themselves being joggled about, Helen

and Nigel braced their feet and linked their fingers as the men staggered with the weight of the carpet and the rolling of the boat.

Suddenly the movement got easier and Helen and Nigel felt themselves being lowered to the ground.

"Is that the carpet I ordered?" demanded a woman's voice.

"It is the one blessed by the goddess, Isis, before your voyage, Great Queen," replied another man's voice.

"Show it to me then," replied the woman, impatiently. "For I must win that Roman general to my cause before the night is out."

The next moment Nigel and Helen tumbled out into bright light and found themselves face to face with Cleopatra, Queen of Egypt!

Everyone froze. In that slow-motion moment, all Helen remembered thinking was how tiny Cleopatra was and how extraordinary she looked.

Her eyes were
enormous and
painted all round
with a thick black
line, and she
wore a crown of
gold leaves.

Helen shrank
back. Cleopatra was staring at them with
a strange glittery look in her eye. It was
almost as if she was expecting them.

"Isis be thanked!" cried Cleopatra. "Your
messengers have arrived. Now Mark
Anthony will be mine!"

She stepped down from her throne and
moved towards Helen and Nigel, who
were sprawled in a heap on the carpet.

"Caution, Great Queen!" cried a guard.
"They may be impostors!"

"They may be demons," shouted

another guard, waving his sword.

"Now what are we going to do?" muttered Nigel. He looked around him. They were on the top deck of a huge boat. All around them was the brightest blue sea he had ever seen.

"Don't move," whispered Helen. "Stay exactly where you are."

But Nigel wasn't listening. If there was no escape they had to tackle things head on. Nigel clambered to his feet. "Let me explain," he said. "We're..."

A curved silver sword swung above his head.

"Get *down*!" Helen shouted. She grabbed Nigel's foot and yanked him to the floor.

Nobody spoke. All you could hear was the slap and gurgle of water along the side of the boat.

A new voice spoke. It was oily and low and Helen didn't like it at all. "Their costumes are most unusual for messengers of the sun goddess."

A woman dressed in scarlet and white left a group of people who stood on one side. Her eyes were like black beads and her thin red lips looked like cuts in her face.

"Don't be foolish, Ishtar," replied Cleopatra. "And they cannot be demons. Demons have no memory. These messengers know of me."

"How so, Great Queen?" replied Ishtar, lightly. If she was angry at being insulted, she didn't let it show.

Cleopatra laughed. "Because, my noble Ishtar, I myself once arrived within a carpet to surprise the Emperor, Julius Caesar." She waved a jewelled hand at Helen and Nigel. "These messengers pay me a compliment by doing the same."

Cleopatra smiled at Helen and Nigel, who were still crouched on the carpet. "Besides, their fiery hair tells me they are from the sun goddess herself."

The woman called Ishtar grunted. "Their actions will prove their identity," she said coldly.

"Indeed they will," cried Cleopatra. She placed her jewelled hands lightly on the children's heads. "Rise and welcome to the royal barge of Cleopatra, Queen of Egypt."

Helen and Nigel looked quickly at one another as they scrambled to their feet.

They were both thinking the same thing.

What should they say now?

If they told Cleopatra the truth she would think they were crazy. She might even want to show them off like exhibits at a freak show. Or she might have them killed.

If they pretended they were indeed messengers from the sun goddess, they would soon be found out and killed anyway.

Helen shivered. She seemed to remember a lot of killing went on in Egyptian times.

Nigel opened his mouth first. "Great Queen," he said bowing low. "We are travellers from another time. We..."

"Do not explain," replied Cleopatra firmly. "I have often heard the sun goddess dwells in other times."

She smiled at their flushed shiny faces. "Indeed I have heard she can hide behind the moon where it is cooler."

Nigel frowned and looked sideways at Helen. "Do you think she means an eclipse?"

A trickle of sweat ran down Helen's face. "I think she's saying we look hot in our clothes," she muttered.

"The girl messenger speaks my mind," said Cleopatra. She looked thoughtfully at both of them and suddenly she seemed unsure. "Indeed your costumes are, ah, most unusual."

The woman called Ishtar sensed the change and moved forward quickly.

Helen thought fast. Their baggy combat trousers and hooded tops must look really strange. Not to mention the purple suede trainers Nigel had put on after school. She glanced at Ishtar. A triumphant smile was spreading across her face. Helen knew she had to say something convincing. "Great Queen," she murmured. "Our strange clothes are to keep us warm for we have been travelling through the cold night skies."

Ishtar made an impatient noise but Cleopatra seemed relieved.

"Please accept my hospitality," she said. "I have great need of your powers and time is short."

She clapped her hands and two servants immediately appeared at her side.

"We will meet again, shortly," she murmured. Then she signalled the servants to come forward.

Nigel and Helen knew they had no choice. They bowed and were instantly led away.

Chapter 4

To Helen's surprise the deck was almost empty when the servant brought her back.

There was no sign of Cleopatra or her followers anywhere. All that was left was the carpet and a small table.

And two guards who stood on the deck.

Helen looked up at their hooded eyes and stony faces. Nothing in their expression would have told her she looked completely different from the girl who had rolled out of Cleopatra's carpet.

She was dressed like a daughter of an Egyptian noble family. She wore a loose white gown embroidered with gold thread and her red hair was braided with gold ribbon.

Helen looked around at the empty deck. Cleopatra had been so desperate for their help. Why would she suddenly disappear?

A nasty feeling prickled Helen's skin. Maybe that horrible woman Ishtar had more power than she let on. Maybe she had convinced Cleopatra that the messengers from the sun goddess should not be trusted after all.

Helen bit her lip. Where was Nigel?

"Hi! Helen!"

It was Nigel's voice but she couldn't see him anywhere.

Nigel sailed past on the end of a rope and landed with a thump on the deck. He stared at Helen as if he couldn't believe his eyes. "Wow! You look amazing!"

Helen ran her hands over her braids. For the first time, ever, she really was pleased with the way she looked. She grinned despite herself.

"What are you grinning about?" asked Nigel.

Helen laughed. "If you must know, I like my hair and..." She blushed. Nigel was wearing a green tunic and gold sandals. "You look pretty good, yourself."

"Have you got the disc safe?" he asked.

"It's in a purse hidden inside my dress," Helen said. Suddenly, she caught the guards' stare and stopped smiling. "Nigel," she whispered. She turned so the guards couldn't see her face. "Those guards are watching every move we make. And there's no sign of Cleopatra anywhere."

"Just look as if you don't care," muttered Nigel under his breath.

They walked over to the side of the boat. They were anchored out in the middle of a harbour. All around them little cargo vessels with square sails moved back and forth over the water. Each one had a pair of eyes painted on the prow.

It seemed to Helen they were being watched by a swarm of water insects. "Something's happened," she whispered to Nigel. She shivered. "There's a nasty feeling around."

Nigel patted her lightly on the arm. "Don't worry. As long as Cleopatra thinks we're messengers from Isis, we're safe."

Helen pulled a face. "But what happens if she doesn't anymore?"

Nigel didn't reply. He was shading his eyes and staring intently at a fleet of boats tied up at the far end of the harbour.

They were different from the wide lumpy barges around them. These boats were sleek and dangerous-looking. Each one bristled with a double row of oars.

Somewhere he had seen boats like that before.

"Your instructions, fabled messengers," demanded a smooth, oily voice. "The Queen awaits them in her chamber." Nigel

and Helen nearly jumped out their skins.

The woman called Ishtar was standing behind them.

Helen stared at Nigel. She hadn't a clue what to say. Worse than that, she was worried in case she said something that would give them away and they would be taken prisoner.

Nigel thought as quickly as he could. What was it Cleopatra had said while they were inside the carpet? *I would win that Roman general to my cause before the night is out.*

Suddenly he knew exactly what kind of boats were tied up at the far end of the harbour. They were Roman fighting ships. Mark Anthony was here with his army and Cleopatra wanted him on her side.

"I've got it!" he croaked.

"What?" hissed Helen.

Nigel pulled Helen towards him. He tried to ignore Ishtar's darkening face and whispered as quickly as he could.

"Mark Anthony is here with his army. Cleopatra wants to win him over. She thinks we know how."

Helen's mind went blank. "Do we?" she whispered. "I mean, do you?"

"Silence!" snapped Ishtar. Her voice went soft and nasty. "If you are who you say you are, you will know exactly how to help the Queen. If, however, you are impostors..."

Ishtar's thin lips parted in a sharp-toothed smiled.

Panic flashed up a picture in Helen's mind. It was the only page of the only history book she had ever read about Cleopatra.

It was about a party she had given for Mark Anthony. It was an extraordinary party which had won him and his army over to Cleopatra's side. Helen bit her lip and tried to stay calm.

All she had to do was remember the details.

She couldn't.

She had to play for time so she could talk to Nigel on his own.

Helen stared at Ishtar's thin red lips. She didn't want to look into her eyes. "You will have your instructions," she said slowly. "Bring us paper and ink and we will write them down."

Nigel's face was
going greyer and greyer.
He rubbed his hands over his face. "I hope
you know what you're doing," he muttered.

To Helen's horror, Ishtar made a signal
to the guard who immediately put a scroll
of parchment, an ink bottle and a long
feathery quill on the small table where the
throne had been.

"Your instructions," hissed Ishtar. Her
beady eyes flickered like a hungry snake
between their faces. She glanced
sideways at the guards.

"Or your sacrifice," she snarled.

Something snapped in Helen's mind.
How dare this horrible woman threaten
them?

Helen spun round and stamped her foot.
"You will not address messengers of the

sun goddess in such a way," she said in a cold furious voice. "You will have our instructions when we are ready."

Then she dragged Nigel over to the side of the deck.

He had no idea what she was up to. Only that it was extremely dangerous.

"Helen," he croaked. "Are you crazy?"

"Shh!" whispered Helen, quickly. "All we have to do is describe the first party Cleopatra put on for Mark Anthony."

Nigel rubbed his hand across his forehead. "What are you talking about?"

"Listen!" said Helen urgently. "You said those boats are Roman fighting ships. We know Mark Anthony is here. History says Cleopatra wanted him on her side so she threw an amazing party. After that, he fell in love with her and didn't go back to Rome."

Nigel stared at Helen's face. Maybe she hadn't flipped out after all. "How do you know that?"

"Because it's on the only page I read in my history book." muttered Helen. "The only problem is I can't remember the details of the party." She paused and took a deep breath. "But I bet you can."

Thoughts whirled round Nigel's mind. He went through all the history books he had read, and he had read a lot of them. Suddenly he saw the page he needed. There was a picture of a ship's deck painted in gold and covered with rose petals.

"I've got it," croaked Nigel for the second time. "It's the one with the rose petals!"

"Rose petals?" repeated

Helen stupidly. Where had they seen rose petals?

They both looked at the carpet at the same moment!

Hundreds of rose petals were woven all over it! So were flowers and ribbons and Roman fighting ships. There were tables covered with food and pictures of boars roasting over great fires.

And in the middle was a Queen.

The carpet was a picture of the party Cleopatra gave for Mark Anthony!

All Helen and Nigel had to do was describe what they saw under their feet.

The rest was history!

But something went wrong.

Someone grabbed them from behind and the next moment the world went black.

Chapter 5

Helen opened her eyes. She knew they were on land, in a cellar. Opposite her Nigel was slumped against the wall. He looked as if he was asleep.

A door creaked. Out of the corner of her eye, Helen saw two people creeping down a flight of steps towards her. One wore a scarlet and white dress. The other had a sword which glittered in the half light.

Helen's heart began to bang like a road drill. It was that horrible woman Ishtar with one of her guards! What could she do? There was no time to warn Nigel and there was nowhere to run.

Helen did the only thing she could think of. She closed her eyes and pretended she was asleep.

"The reign of Cleopatra is over," Ishtar's voice was low and triumphant. "Without the help of these messengers, the Roman general will leave on the morning tide."

She prodded Helen's legs with her foot and laughed a nasty laugh. "At last, my brother will be king."

"What shall I do with them?" muttered the guard.

"Keep them," replied Ishtar. "I will exhibit them to my brother's army tomorrow. After that—" she paused. "We will feed them to the fish."

There was a swish of material and the sound of footsteps fading away.

The door closed.

Helen opened her eyes and let them travel slowly around the room. It was the only way to keep down the panic that was clutching at her throat. She tried to think how they had got there but she didn't have a clue. All she could remember was the feel of strong arms pinning her hands. Then a strange-smelling hood had been pulled over her head. It must have been soaked in some potion because she had immediately fallen asleep.

"Helen."

Helen nearly jumped out of her skin.

"Nigel," she croaked.

"Shh! Don't talk so loud."

"Did you hear what Ishtar said?"

"Every word."

"What are we going to do?"

Nigel looked up. Light was streaming through two squares cut high in the wall. If he stood on something, he would be able to see out.

"I'm going to find out where we are," Nigel tiptoed across the room and picked up a large pottery urn.

He turned it upside down, and, holding on to a lump of stone that was sticking out of the wall, he heaved himself up.

"What can you see?" whispered Helen.

"Cleopatra's boat at anchor," replied Nigel. His voice dropped to a low whisper. "We'll never get back to it."

"Let me see."

They swapped places. Helen looked all along the shore line. There were lots of little boats bobbing at their moorings. *Little boats with sails.*

"We'll sail back," she said firmly. "All we have to do is get out of here."

Nigel took the stopper out of one of the pottery jars. He put his finger inside. It was full of oil. Slippery, slimy oil.

"I know what we'll do," he whispered. Helen turned round. She could see his teeth shining white in his face.

Five minutes later, they were ready. A river of oil flowed down the stairs. Nigel was crouched at the top. All Helen had to do was yodel at the top of her voice, and when the door opened, Nigel would give the guard a little shove.

Oil and gravity would take care of the rest.

Everything worked according to plan.

Ten minutes later, Nigel was up to his waist shoving a tiny boat through warm muddy water.

On board, Helen unfurled a square tan sail as quickly as she could. She pulled the rudder towards her and hoped against hope for a puff of wind.

Suddenly the sail filled.

"Now!" shouted Helen.

Nigel clambered over the side and landed in a black muddy heap in the bottom of the boat.

Once again they heard the sound of

water gurgling past the hull.

Only this time, it was the most wonderful sound in the world!

All around them men in boats shouted to each other. Some were carrying fruit and vegetables. Others were pulling fat silver fish out of the water. None of them seemed interested in the little boat racing over the waves with a red-haired girl at the tiller and a red-headed boy crouched at the prow.

Suddenly Helen thought of their so-called history project and the rest of their class.

She thought of Rhona McVeigh playing Cleopatra and Sophie wearing arm bands and a curly wig, pretending to be Mark Anthony. She laughed and shook her head. "They'll never believe us, you know," she said.

Nigel knew exactly what she meant. He grinned and wiped a smear of mud from his face. "Never in 41 years BC!"

"Is that what year it is?"

"That's what I think it says in the history books."

Helen pushed the rudder away. The sail swung round and the little boat slid over the top of a wave. The wind had picked up and they were moving quickly now.

Ahead of them, Cleopatra's royal barge glittered like a great golden swan.

As Helen and Nigel got closer and closer, they could see lots of people running up and down the side. They seemed to be waving.

"Do you think they look friendly?" shouted Helen over rush of the wind and the slap of the waves.

Nigel held up two pairs of crossed fingers. "They'd better be," he yelled. "It's our last chance!"

It was Cleopatra's last chance, too. Ishtar's treachery had taken the Queen completely unawares. She had given Cleopatra a sleeping potion just before she had come on deck to question Helen and Nigel. When Cleopatra awoke, her messengers had been kidnapped and all her servants had been sent away.

Now Cleopatra welcomed Helen and Nigel with open arms, but her eyes were hard. She needed their instructions

immediately or else all would be lost.

Helen and Nigel knew exactly what to say. They sat down and described to the last detail the party Cleopatra would give for Mark Anthony that very evening.

"Are you sure this is the way to win Mark Anthony to my cause?" asked Cleopatra finally. Two teams of servants had filled scroll after scroll with instructions.

Cleopatra sat back on her throne. "Even I have never heard of such extravagance."

But Helen and Nigel were firm. The boat's sails must be purple and drenched with perfume. The decks must be knee deep in rose petals. There must be meat cooked with coriander, cumin and poppy seeds. Eight wild boar must be set to roast over fires at different times. Only that way could the Roman guests be sure to have meat that was perfectly cooked whenever they were hungry.

"And for dessert?" croaked the servant in charge of food.

"There must be figs, grapes, pomegranates and cakes soaked in honey," replied Nigel immediately.

Cleopatra looked at Helen. "And have the messengers of Isis any instruction as to my costume?" She tossed her glossy braids and played with the gold snake necklace at her throat. "I usually wear white."

In her mind Helen saw the words written in her history book, 'Cleopatra lay on a couch under a gold canopy. Her crew were beautiful girls. Little boys pretended they were Cupids. She herself was dressed as the goddess Venus. Mark Anthony didn't have a chance'.

Helen hid a smile. She wasn't sure about the last line but the rest of it was real. She cleared her throat. "Do you have a team of dressmakers, Great Queen?"

At that moment a wizened old man trotted across the deck and whispered something in Cleopatra's ear.

Helen and Nigel held their breath. The old man must be very important to be allowed to interrupt the meeting. What was he saying? Would they find themselves prisoners again?

Cleopatra bowed her head as the old man spoke. "And is she secure?" she asked at last.

The old man nodded, kissed the Queen's hand and trotted back across the deck.

Cleopatra slumped back in relief.

"Great news," she announced. "Ishtar has been captured. Her brother's army has deserted him."

She walked into the middle of deck and clapped her hands. "Let the preparations for the party begin!"

Helen and Nigel exchanged looks. So far so good but they both knew time was running out for them, too.

Chapter 6

It's amazing what can be done if you have
enough servants, thought Helen later.

In the space of hours, the royal barge
was transformed. And strangest of all,
even though neither Helen nor Nigel
actually helped lay things out, everything
looked exactly like the picture
woven on the carpet.

The carpet itself had been especially adorned.

Something like an elaborate bird cage rose over the top of it. The framework was decorated with flowers and climbing vines. Inside a little oil lamp was burning.

It had been turned into an altar to the goddess Isis. Helen and Nigel stood on deck and waited nervously for Mark Anthony to arrive. Something had changed in Cleopatra. Now that everything was ready, she seemed to have forgotten their help. Instead of asking their advice, she gave them orders. They were to stay by her throne and await further instructions.

Suddenly there was a tremendous sound of trumpets and a clash of cymbals.

Roman soldiers lined up to form a guard of honour. The next moment a man wearing a scarlet cloak over silver chest armour strode on to the deck. He was short and thickset with dark curly hair. His face was stern and square but as he looked about him, his eyes went wide with amazement.

"Mark Anthony be praised!" sang a high ringing voice.

At that moment, a different kind of music filled the air. It was sweet and beautiful and full of mystery.

Cleopatra, Queen of Egypt, was carried on to the deck on a huge litter hung with cloth of gold. She wore a gown of cotton, embroidered with pearls and shimmering hearts. Her glossy black braids were piled up under a glittering headdress of rubies and diamonds. She had turned herself into Venus, the goddess of love.

Mark Anthony stepped forward. "Great Queen," he cried. "I am honoured beyond words."

Then he kissed her hand and from that moment on, he never took his eyes off her face.

It was the party to end all parties. There was feasting and dancing and music making until night, and the sky twinkled with a million stars.

Cleopatra charmed her guests with smiles and easy laughter but all the while she insisted that Nigel and Helen stay by her side.

Suddenly, Mark Anthony made his way
to Cleopatra's platform and bowed in front
of Helen and Nigel. "Our Great Queen
does me a special favour," he said as he
raised a golden goblet. "Such wisdom as
yours will be a huge asset in Rome."

Helen eyes went round and terrified. She

opened her mouth to speak but the look
on Nigel's face told her to keep quiet.

"Indeed, general," said Nigel smoothly.

"When do you travel?"

Mark Anthony drank deeply from his goblet. "Not I, messengers of Isis. It is you who will sail on the morning tide."

Cleopatra sat up and rested her jewelled hand lightly on Mark Anthony's arm. Her eyes met Nigel's and held them. "The messengers of Isis will do my bidding," she said slowly.

As she spoke, a group of Roman soldiers made their way across the deck towards them. They stopped at the edge of the platform and saluted.

Mark Anthony turned to Helen and Nigel. "Your guard of honour comes to escort you to my ship."

Helen's eyes slid sideways to the corner of the deck where the carpet lay. Somehow they had to get to it.

"Great Queen," she murmured. "The

messengers of Isis are pleased to do your bidding." She stood up. "But first we must give thanks to our goddess for her help."

Nigel followed her gaze and understood what she was trying to do. He stood up quickly. "Allow us this moment with our goddess, Great Queen." He bowed low. "Her blessing will favour your success."

Cleopatra played with a rope of pearls that hung around her neck. "The goddess has no need of your thanks," she replied coldly. "I have made her an altar. That is enough."

Mark Anthony put down his goblet and took Cleopatra's hand. "Grant their request, Great Queen," he murmured. "A goddess may be thanked more than once."

Cleopatra hesitated. It was as if she suspected something but could not understand why she should feel suspicious.

"Go," she said at last. "But do not tarry. Your services to me are over. The general has need of you, now."

Helen and Nigel bowed. As they walked across the deck, the whole boat fell silent.

Helen thought she was going to faint. "What if she changes her mind?" she whispered.

They were only a few steps from the carpet...

"Keep walking," muttered Nigel. "And get the disk out of your purse."

Helen slipped her hand inside her dress and held the disc in her fingers.

It must have been the movement of her hand.

Suddenly Cleopatra jumped to her feet. "Seize them!" she shrieked.

Then everything happened at once.

Helen pulled the disc from her purse as Nigel dragged her on to the carpet.

A curved sword slashed through the wooden framework of the birdcage. Vines and flowers tumbled to the ground.

Helen heard herself scream.

She felt the disc being pulled from her hand. She screamed again.

Then everything started to spin.

It went faster and faster and faster.

Helen remembered a blur of gold. She remembered Nigel's arm around her shoulder and his voice in her ear. "It's all right. We're safe."

Then the world went black and silver. It felt as if they were falling in a deep, dark sky through a shower of shooting stars.

Nigel and Helen sat cross legged on the Turkish carpet and stared at each other. They were in the attic. Afternoon sunlight poured through a skylight in the roof.

It looked as if nothing had happened at all. They were both wearing baggy trousers and hooded tops. Nigel's purple trainers were still brand new. But they knew everything had changed and nothing would ever be the same again.

Out of the corner of her eye, Helen saw the open door of the big cupboard and the glittery dresses and fancy old suits that hung over the top.

Her mind went right back to what they had been talking about before Nigel had dragged out the carpet. A crazy idea popped into her head. She could hardly believe that she had even thought of it. She pulled down the clothes and held them up in front of her.

"Rhona McVeigh's Fancy-Dress Disco," said Nigel with a grin.

"Exactly," cried Helen.

Nigel jumped up and his eyes were sparkling. "Brilliant," he cried. "As long as you braid your hair with gold ribbon!"

Both of them burst out laughing.

Then they danced round around the carpet.

"It's true!" cried Helen.

"What's true?" shouted Nigel.

Helen threw back her head and let out a whoop of delight.

"Things really are different for redheads!"